for
Miss Penny Rose
Great Auntie Mary
from

Good-bye, Bumps!

Talking to What's Bugging You

Illustrated by
Stacy Heller Budnick

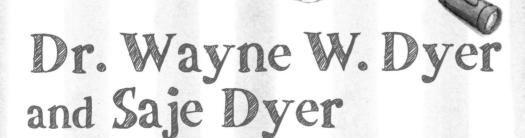

Dr. Wayne W. Dyer
and Saje Dyer

HAY HOUSE, INC.
Carlsbad, California • New York City
London • Sydney • Johannesburg
Vancouver • Hong Kong • New Delhi

Published and distributed in the United States by: Hay House, Inc.: www.hayhouse.com® • *Published and distribued in Australia by:* Hay House Australia Pty. Ltd.: www.hayhouse.com.au • *Published and distributed in the United Kingdom by:* Hay House UK, Ltd.: www.hayhouse.co.uk • *Published and distributed in the Republic of South Africa by:* Hay House SA (Pty), Ltd.: www.hayhouse.co.za • *Distributed in Canada by:* Raincoast Books: www.raincoast.com • *Published in India by:* Hay House Publishers India: www.hayhouse.co.in

Editorial assistance: Kristina Tracy and Jenny Richards • *Interior design:* Jenny Richards • *Illustrations:* © Stacy Heller Budnick

Library of Congress Control Number: 2013955834

ISBN: 978-1-4019-4585-5

17 16 15 14   4 3 2 1

1st edition, February 2014

To my beautiful daughter Saje, thank you for
sharing your wonderful story with the world.
I love you.

—Wayne Dyer

I would like dedicate this book to my father and
mother, Wayne and Marcelene Dyer, who gave me
the wisdom to know that I can always heal myself!

—Saje Dyer

I'm going to tell you a story about something that happened to me.
It's pretty amazing—you might even wonder how it can be true—but it is!
Have you ever had something that bugged you a lot? Well, I did . . .

When I was five I had these bumps on my face.
They felt icky and they really bothered me.
I thought about them all the time.

My mom and dad took me to the doctor.
The doctor said I could take some medicine, or
I could wait and they might go away on their own.

I decided to wait and see.
So, I waited . . .

and waited . . .

and waited . . . but they were still there.
My bumps were making me mad!

One day, I was stomping around the house, pouting about my bumps. My dad said, "Hey, those bumps sure seem to be making you unhappy. I have an interesting idea that you could try . . . maybe you could talk to your bumps."

"What do you mean?" I asked.

"Well," Dad said, "look in the mirror and really talk to them. Out loud. Say something like, 'Hi, bumps, maybe there is a reason you are here. Thanks for coming, but I am ready for you to go now. And whether you stay or go, I am done feeling bad about you.'"

It sounded weird, but my dad is a smart guy and by then I was willing to try anything. . . .

So that night I crawled under my covers with a flashlight and had a little chat with my bumps. I said, "I don't know why you are here, but I would really like you to leave. I'm letting you go—good-bye, bumps!"

I did this every night for a week, and one morning when I reached up to touch my face, I couldn't believe it . . . my bumps! They were gone!

I couldn't wait to tell my dad. "Look, Dad, it worked! They're gone!" I shouted. "What's the trick? Does it work for anything else?"

Dad smiled and said, "It's not a trick—
it's just a way of thinking about things—
and yes, it works for lots of stuff."

"Think of your cousin Curtie. He is very shy. If you were shy like him, you could say to yourself: *Hey, self, I know you are shy. There is nothing wrong with that, and I know it is a part of me. But I am ready to say good-bye to being shy and feeling bad about it.*"

"Now, you wouldn't instantly become not shy at all, but as you change your feelings about being shy, you will begin to notice a difference in the way you act."

"Sometimes, you may not be able to change something—maybe you were born with it. I am a good example of that. When I was younger, I didn't like my freckles. I had millions of them. I wasted a lot of my time thinking about them and wishing they would magically disappear. Then one day, I decided to let go of my bad feelings about my freckles and make peace with the fact that they are a part of who I am. After a while, I even started to like them a little bit!"

"Now of course, some things that people were born with they can change, right? Look at Ally here—she wanted her teeth to be straight, so she did something about it—she got braces."

"But whether you can change something or not,
the point is: Stop giving it power over you. That means,
don't let it be the most important, biggest thing in
your life, and you will notice some changes.

"Maybe your bumps went away because you talked
to them and they listened. You would be surprised how
much your body works together with your mind."

Later, in my room, I thought about everything Dad had said and decided to write it down.

What to do when something is bugging me

What to do when something is bugging me:

1.   Say hello to whatever is bothering me. Understand that it is a part of me whether I want it to be or not.

2.   Let go of bad feelings about the thing I don't like.

3.   Don't let something that bugs me have power over me (I give it power by making it important!).

4.   Remind myself that I will feel better and happier if I don't let my problems have power over me.

5.   Change what I can—and if I can't, then try to change the way I feel about it.

So that's it for my story. I hope it helps you when you have something that is bugging you a lot. Maybe you worry too much, or you think your ears are too big, or maybe you even have some bumps, too. Just try talking to what bugs you and see what happens!

Dear Parents,

We hope you and your child have enjoyed this true story from Saje's childhood. She has shared it with several audiences when speaking at my lectures and got a terrific response. So, we decided to write this book to share the story with as many people as possible.

As we have tried to explain in this book, it is often more about the "power" we give things (i.e., bumps) than the actual thing (bumps) that causes us so much pain and/or worry.

If we could all have the faith of a child and truly believe that our "bumps" will go away if we just ask, it really can happen . . . and it has.

Everyone's situation is different. If your child has something that is unlikely to go away—perhaps something they were born with—remember, the point of this story is that acknowledging our problem can take away the power we have given it. And that can be a huge relief no matter what a child is facing.

Yes, there are some things that none of us can change or make go away, but taking the focus off of "it" really does make a difference.

We sincerely hope that you and your child gain something from reading about Saje's experience and will be able to use this lesson to help in some small (or big) way in your lives.

Wayne and Saje Dyer

We hope you enjoyed this Hay House book. If you'd like to receive our online catalog featuring additional information on Hay House books and products, or if you'd like to find out more about the Hay Foundation, please contact:

Hay House, Inc.
P.O. Box 5100
Carlsbad, CA 92018-5100

(760) 431-7695 or (800) 654-5126
(760) 431-6948 (fax) or (800) 650-5115 (fax)
www.hayhouse.com® • www.hayfoundation.org

Published and distributed in Australia by: Hay House Australia Pty. Ltd., 18/36 Ralph St., Alexandria NSW 2015
Phone: 612-9669-4299 • Fax: 612-9669-4144 • www.hayhouse.com.au

Published and distributed in the United Kingdom by: Hay House UK, Ltd., Astley House, 33 Notting Hill Gate, London W11 3JQ
Phone: 44-20-3675-2450 • Fax: 44-20-3675-2451 • www.hayhouse.co.uk

Published and distributed in the Republic of South Africa by: Hay House SA (Pty), Ltd.,
P.O. Box 990, Witkoppen 2068 • Phone/Fax: 27-11-467-8904 • www.hayhouse.co.za

Published in India by: Hay House Publishers India, Muskaan Complex, Plot No. 3, B-2, Vasant Kunj,
New Delhi 110 070 • Phone: 91-11-4176-1620 • Fax: 91-11-4176-1630 • www.hayhouse.co.in

Distributed in Canada by: Raincoast Books, 2440 Viking Way, Richmond, B.C. V6V 1N2
Phone: 1-800-663-5714 • Fax: 1-800-565-3770 • www.raincoast.com